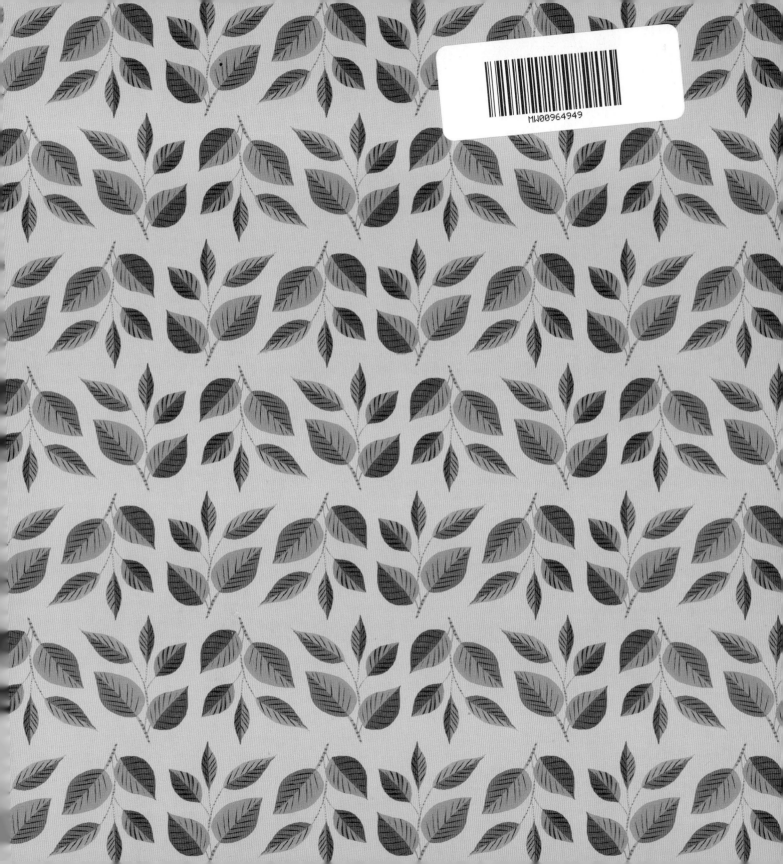

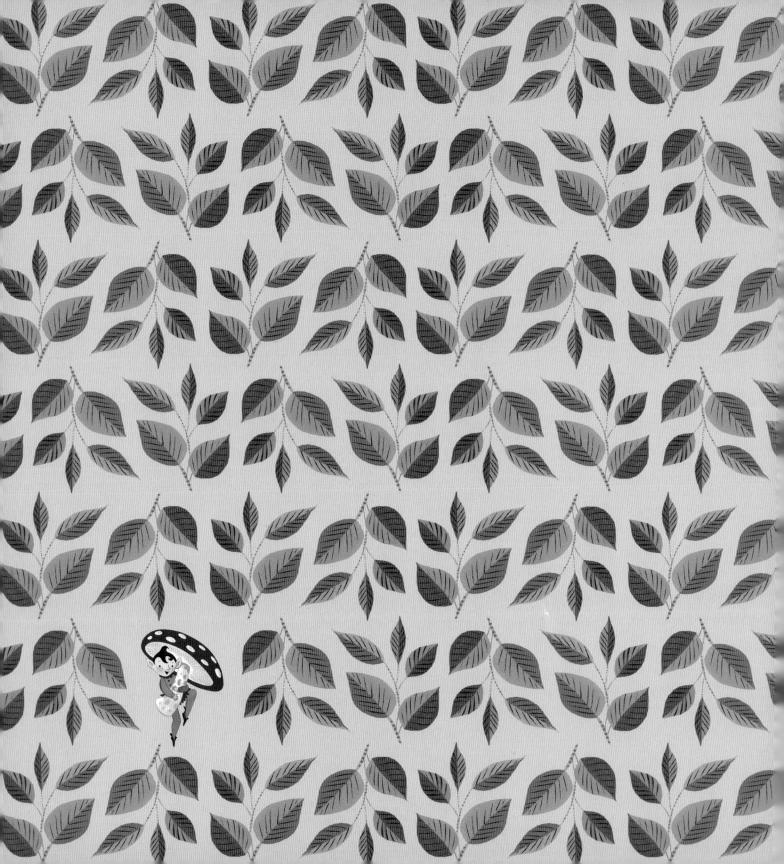

This Book Belongs to

_____

A Children's Treasury of
Poems

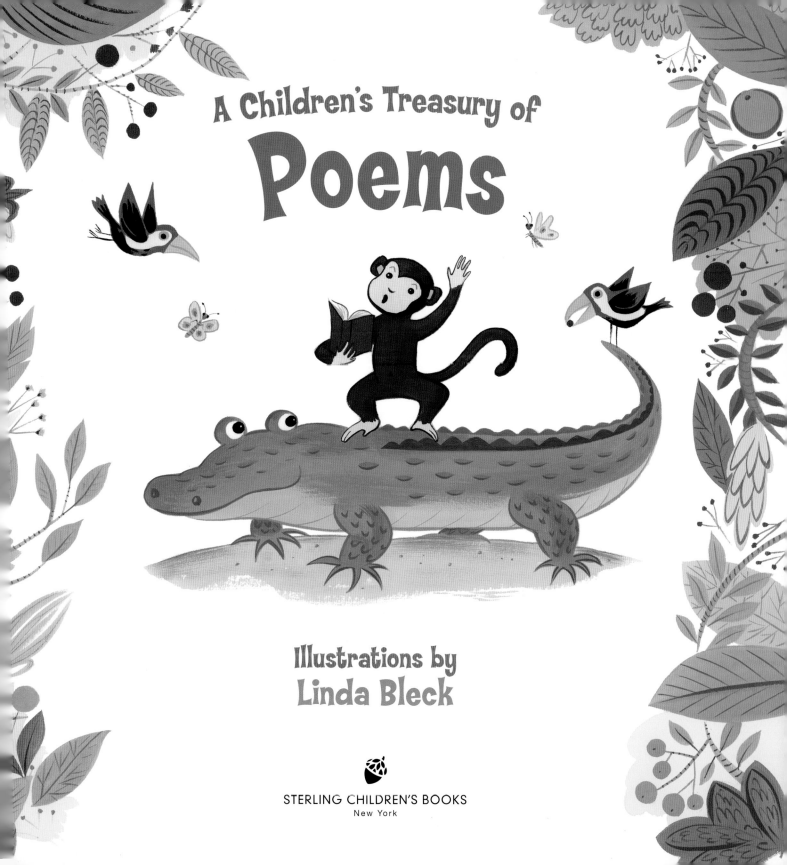

Illustrations by
Linda Bleck

STERLING CHILDREN'S BOOKS
New York

Bed in Summer

by Robert Louis Stevenson

In winter I get up at night
And dress by yellow candle-light.
In summer quite the other way,
I have to go to bed by day.

I have to go to bed and see
The birds still hopping on the tree,
Or hear the grown-up people's feet
Still going past me in the street.

And does it not seem hard to you,
When all the sky is clear and blue,
And I should like so much to play,
To have to go to bed by day?

The Man in the Moon

Anonymous

The Man in the Moon as he sails the sky
Is a very remarkable skipper,
But he made a mistake when he tried to take
A drink of milk from the Dipper.
He dipped right out of the Milky Way,
And slowly and carefully filled it,
The Big Bear growled, and the Little Bear howled
And frightened him so that he spilled it!

Who Likes the Rain?

by Clara Doty Bates

"I," said the duck, "I call it fun,
For I have my little red rubbers on;
They make a cunning three-toed track
In the soft, cool mud. Quack! Quack!"

"I!" cried the dandelion, "I!
My roots are thirsty, my buds are dry."
And she lifted a tousled yellow head
Out of her green and grassy bed.

"I hope 'twill pour! I hope 'twill pour!"
Purred the tree-toad at his gray back door.
"For, with a broad leaf for a roof,
I am perfectly weatherproof."

Sang the brook: "I laugh at every drop,
And wish they never need to stop,
Till a big river I grew to be,
And could find my way to the sea."

"I," shouted Ted, "for I can run,
With my high-top boots and my rain-coat on,
Through every puddle and runlet and pool
That I find on my way to school."

The Little Turtle

by Vachel Lindsay

There was a little turtle.
He lived in a box.
He swam in a puddle.
He climbed on the rocks.

He snapped at a mosquito.
He snapped at a flea.
He snapped at a minnow.
And he snapped at me.

He caught the mosquito.
He caught the flea.
He caught the minnow.
But he didn't catch me.

How Doth the Little Crocodile

by *Lewis Carroll*

How doth the little crocodile
Improve his shining tail,
And pour the waters of the Nile
On every golden scale!

How cheerfully he seems to grin,
How neatly spreads his claws,
And welcomes little fishes in,
With gently smiling jaws!

The Dream Fairy

by Thomas Hood

A little fairy comes at night,
Her eyes are blue, her hair is brown,
With silver spots upon her wings,
And from the moon she flutters down.

She has a little silver wand,
And when a good child goes to bed,
She waves her wand from left to right,
And makes a circle round her head.

And then it dreams of pleasant things,
Of fountains filled with fairy fish,
And trees that bear delicious fruit,
And bow their branches at a wish;

Of arbours filled with dainty scents
From lovely flowers that never fade,
Bright flies that glitter in the sun,
And glow-worms shining in the shade;

And talking birds with gifted tongues
For singing songs and telling tales,
And pretty dwarfs to show the way
Through fairy hills and fairy dales.

The Floorless Room

by Gelett Burgess

I Wish that my Room had a Floor!

I don't so Much Care for a Door,

But this Crawling Around

Without Touching the Ground

Is Getting to be Quite a Bore!

The Purple Cow

by Gelett Burgess

I never saw a Purple Cow,

I never hope to see one;

But I can tell you, anyhow,

I'd rather see than be one!

The Owl and the Pussycat

by Edward Lear

The Owl and the Pussycat went to sea
In a beautiful pea green boat;
They took some honey, and plenty of money,
Wrapped up in a five pound note.
The Owl looked up to the stars above,
And sang to a small guitar,
"O lovely Pussy, O Pussy, my love,
What a beautiful Pussy you are,
You are,
You are!
What a beautiful Pussy you are!"

Pussy said to the Owl, "You elegant fowl!
How charmingly sweet you sing!
O let us be married, too long we have tarried:
But what shall we do for a ring?"
They sailed away, for a year and a day,
To the land where the bong-tree grows
And there in a wood a Piggy-wig stood
With a ring at the end of his nose,
His nose,
His nose,
With a ring at the end of his nose.

"Dear pig, are you willing to sell for one shilling
Your ring?" Said the Piggy, "I will."
So they took it away, and were married next day
By the Turkey who lives on the hill.
They dined on mince, and slices of quince,
Which they ate with a runcible spoon;
And hand in hand, on the edge of the sand,
They danced by the light of the moon,
The moon,
The moon,
They danced by the light of the moon.

The Swing

by Robert Louis Stevenson

How do you like to go up in a swing,
Up in the air so blue?
Oh, I do think it the pleasantest thing
Ever a child can do!

Up in the air and over the wall,
Till I can see so wide,
River and trees and cattle and all
Over the countryside—

Till I look down on the garden green,
Down on the roof so brown—
Up in the air I go flying again,
Up in the air and down!

Animal Crackers

by *Christopher Morley*

Animal crackers, and cocoa to drink,
That is the finest of suppers, I think;
When I'm grown up and can have what I please,
I think I will always insist upon these.

What do you choose when you're offered a treat?
When Mother says, "What would you like best to eat?"
Is it waffles and syrup, or cinnamon toast?
It's cocoa and animal crackers that I love most!

The kitchen's the coziest place I know:
The kettle is singing, the stove is aglow,
And there in the twilight, how jolly to see,
The cocoa and animals waiting for me.

Daddy and Mother dine later with Kate,
With Mary to cook for them, Susan in wait;
But they don't have nearly as much fun as I,
Who eat in the kitchen with Nurse standing by;
And Daddy once said, he would like to be me,
Having cocoa and animals once more for tea!

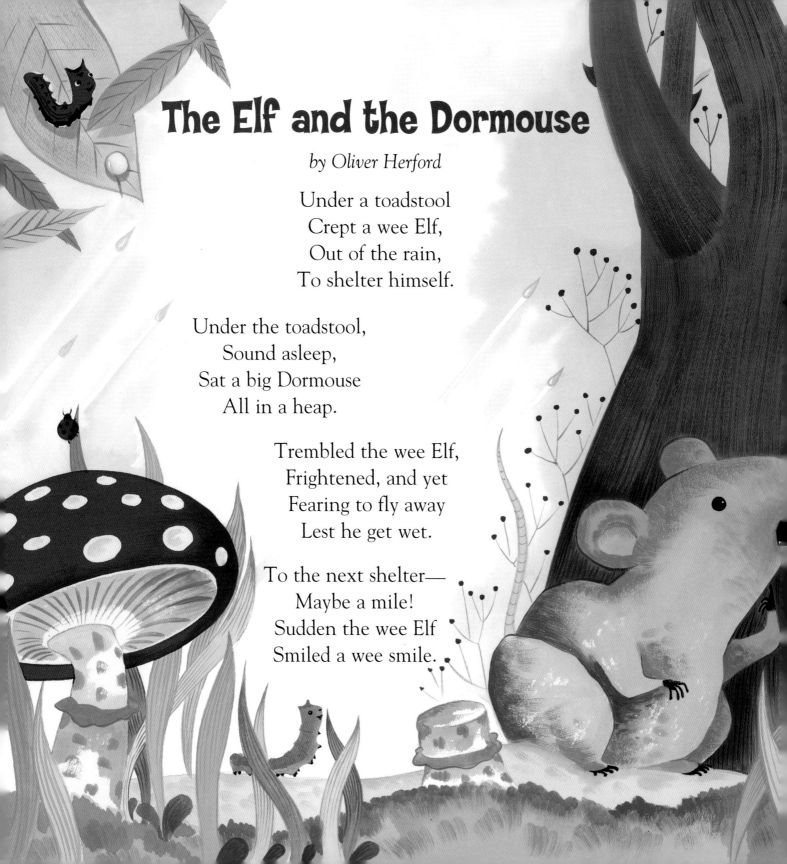

The Elf and the Dormouse

by Oliver Herford

Under a toadstool
Crept a wee Elf,
Out of the rain,
To shelter himself.

Under the toadstool,
Sound asleep,
Sat a big Dormouse
All in a heap.

Trembled the wee Elf,
Frightened, and yet
Fearing to fly away
Lest he get wet.

To the next shelter—
Maybe a mile!
Sudden the wee Elf
Smiled a wee smile.

Tugged till the toadstool
Toppled in two.
Holding it over him,
Gayly he flew.

Soon he was safe home,
Dry as could be.
Soon woke the Dormouse—
"Good gracious me!

Where is my toadstool!"
Loud he lamented.
—And that's how umbrellas
First were invented.

Table Manners

by Gelett Burgess

The Goops they lick their fingers,
And the Goops they lick their knives;
They spill their broth on the tablecloth—

Oh, they lead disgusting lives!
The Goops they talk while eating,
And loud and fast they chew;

And that is why I'm glad that I
Am not a Goop—are you?

The Cats Have Come to Tea

by Kate Greenaway

What did she see—oh, what did she see,
As she stood leaning against the tree?
Why, all the cats had come to tea.

What a fine turnout from roundabout!
All the houses had let them out.
And here they were with scamper and shout.

"Mew–mew–mew!" was all they could say,
And, "We hope we find you well today."

Oh, what should she do—oh, what should she do?
What a lot of milk they would get through;
For here they were with "Mew–mew–mew!"

She didn't know—oh, she didn't know,
If bread and butter they'd like or no;
They might want little mice, oh! oh! oh!

Dear me—oh, dear me,
All the cats had come to tea.

There Was a Young Lady of Bute

by Edward Lear

There was a Young Lady of Bute,
Who played on a silver-gilt flute;
She played several jigs, to her uncle's white pigs,
That amusing Young Lady of Bute.

There Was an Old Man with a Beard

by Edward Lear

There was an Old Man with a beard,
Who said, "It is just as I feared!
Two Owls and a Hen, four Larks and a Wren,
Have all built their nests in my beard."

Mr. Nobody

Anonymous

I know a funny little man,
As quiet as a mouse,
Who does the mischief that is done
In everybody's house!
There's no one ever sees his face,
And yet we all agree,
That every plate we break was cracked
By Mr. Nobody.

'Tis he who always tears our books,
Who leaves the door ajar,
Who pulls the buttons from our shirts,
And scatters pins afar;
That squeaking door will always squeak,
For, prithee, don't you see,
We leave the oiling to be done
By Mr. Nobody.

The finger marks upon the door,
By none of us are made;
We never leave the blinds unclosed,
To let the curtains fade.
The ink we never spill, the boots
That lying round you see,
Are not our boots; they all belong
To Mr. Nobody.

He puts damp wood upon the fire,
That kettles cannot boil;
His are the feet that bring in mud,
And all the carpets soil.
The papers always are mislaid,
Who had them last but he?
There's no one tosses them about
But Mr. Nobody.

A Good Play

by Robert Louis Stevenson

We built a ship upon the stairs
All made of the back-bedroom chairs,
And filled it full of sofa pillows
To go a-sailing on the billows.

We took a saw and several nails,
And water in the nursery pails;
And Tom said, "Let us also take
An apple and a slice of cake";
Which was enough for Tom and me
To go a-sailing on, till tea.

We sailed along for days and days,
And had the very best of plays;
But Tom fell out and hurt his knee,
So there was no one left but me.

I Love My Books

Anonymous

I love my books,
They are the homes
Of queens and fairies,
Knights and gnomes.
Each time I read I make a call
On some quaint person large or small,
Who welcomes me with hearty hand
And leads me through his wonderland.
Each book is like
A city street
Along whose winding
Way I meet
New friends and old who laugh and sing
And take me off adventuring!

For my sister, Susie.
— L.B.

STERLING CHILDREN'S BOOKS
New York

An Imprint of Sterling Publishing
1166 Avenue of the Americas
New York, NY 10036

Illustrations © 2008 by Linda Bleck
Paperback edition published in 2015.
Previously published by Sterling Publishing, Co., Inc. in a different format in 2008.
Designed by Josh Simons, Simonsays Design!

ISBN 978-1-4549-1474-7

Distributed in Canada by Sterling Publishing
c/o Canadian Manda Group, 664 Annette Street
Toronto, Ontario, Canada M6S 2C8
Distributed in the United Kingdom by GMC Distribution Services
Castle Place, 166 High Street, Lewes, East Sussex, England BN7 1XU
Distributed in Australia by Capricorn Link (Australia) Pty. Ltd.
P.O. Box 704, Windsor, NSW 2756, Australia

For information about custom editions, special sales, and premium and corporate purchases,
please contact Sterling Special Sales at 800-805-5489 or specialsales@sterlingpublishing.com.

Manufactured in China
Lot #:
2 4 6 8 10 9 7 5 3 1
01/15

www.sterlingpublishing.com/kids

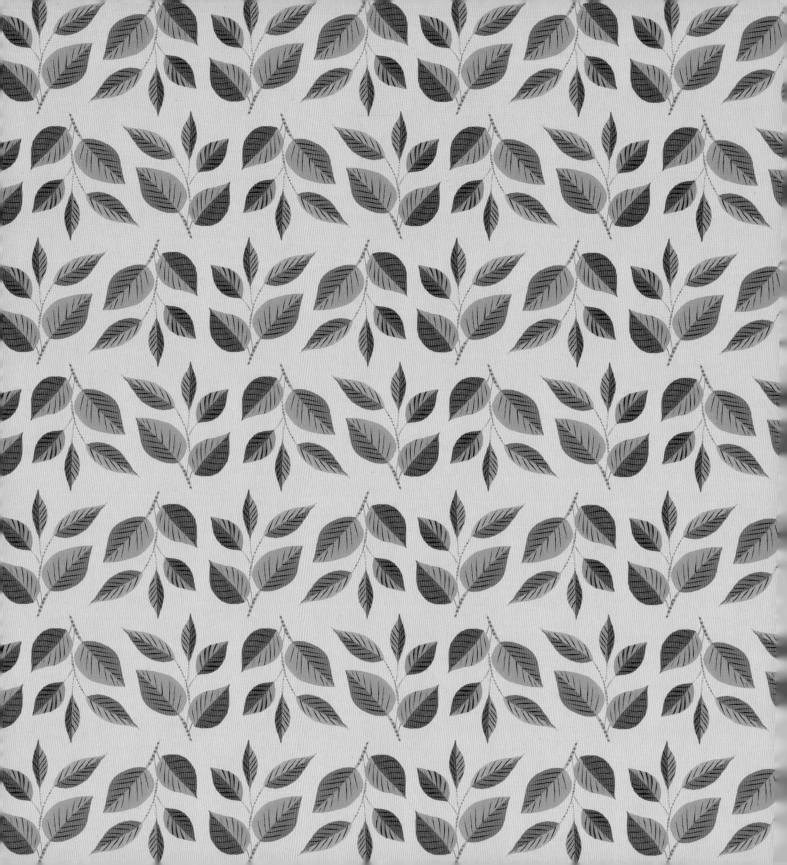